Tia and the Terracotta Horse

Adrita Goswami

Ukiyoto Publishing

All global publishing rights are held by

Ukiyoto Publishing

Published in 2023

Content Copyright © Adrita Goswami

ISBN 9789359207926

All rights reserved.

No part of this publication may be reproduced, transmitted, or stored in a retrieval system, in any form by any means, electronic, mechanical, photocopying, recording or otherwise, without the prior permission of the publisher.

The moral rights of the author have been asserted.

This is a work of fiction. Names, characters, businesses, places, events, locales, and incidents are either the products of the author's imagination or used in a fictitious manner. Any resemblance to actual persons, living or dead, or actual events is purely coincidental.

This book is sold subject to the condition that it shall not by way of trade or otherwise, be lent, resold, hired out or otherwise circulated, without the publisher's prior consent, in any form of binding or cover other than that in which it is published.

www.ukiyoto.com

Dedication

This book is humbly dedicated to all the talented terracotta artisans of India, whose wonderful art deserves more recognition and respect.

Contents

Tia makes a Terracotta Horse	1
Celebrating Rakhi Festival with Tarak	4
Exploring East India	8
Exploring North India	14
Exploring West India	17
Exploring South India	20
About the Author	*24*

Tia makes a Terracotta Horse

Tucked away in the lush countryside of rural Bengal is the beautiful town of Bishnupur, famous for its rich history and heritage. The landscape of Bishnupur is dotted with picturesque lakes, green fields, and magnificent terracotta temples and palaces. As one roams through the town, the view is still strikingly pristine and dated, but for modern buildings and vehicles.

In this cozy village atmosphere, we find Tia Kumbhakar, a happy-go-lucky 10-year-old girl. Her first name which means "parrot" in Bengali is a perfect fit for her bright personality and beautiful features. Her feet are always yearning to run to the field and trees to gaze at the kites and the birds camouflaged in the green trees. Growing up in this setting, Tia can mimic bird calls, and one can often hear the birds calling back to her.

When she is not chasing birds and kites, we can find Tia learning the art of terracotta pottery from her grandmother, Gayatri Devi. Tia feels proud of being the granddaughter of a famed terracotta artisan, whose nimble fingers have shaped masterpieces that adorn living rooms and showcases in luxurious homes across the world. The simple, close-knit Kumbhakar family earns their livelihood through terracotta pottery. Their collection includes various kinds of animals, birds, earthen pots, flower pots, vases, idols of deities, oil lamps, and utensils. Tia receives more attention from her grandmother than from her busy parents, Gangaram and Kamala. She helps in the family business after finishing her daily lessons. Her love for the craft deepened after having a series of wonderful adventures during her last vacation. Let us now go back to the time when Tia made her first terracotta sculpture.

One Sunday evening, Tia was applying the finishing touches on a terracotta horse under a blooming red krishnachura tree in the lingering light of dusk. She had been working on it for almost a month, and she was determined to complete it all by herself. She wanted the horse to look like the magic horses she had read about in her story books. As she was adorning it with the ornaments she had bought at the Rath Yatra fair, her mother called her for dinner. "Just a minute, Maa!" said Tia, impatient to complete her horse.

"Tiaaaa," her mother called again. "Come before the food gets cold, dear."

Tia rushed to the kitchen, bumping against a freshly baked clay pot on the way. To her relief, it fell on the pile of hay. Guilty of having previously broken many clay pots, Tia was relieved to see the pot unbroken.

"When will you learn to be careful, young lady?" her father asked in a tone of affectionate annoyance.

"She is still a child," said Gayatri Devi, who always takes her granddaughter's side.

Little Tia sat on a floral embroidered jute mat between her father and her grandmother. Her mother served them rice, lentils, fish curry, and fried eggplants on terracotta plates and bowls. Although the meal was delicious, Tia ate in a hurry.

"Tia, eat slowly lest you choke on the fish bones," warned her mother.

"Yes, Maa," said Tia, gulping down her glass of water. After washing up, she went back to complete her terracotta horse. When the decoration was finished, the horse looked like it came straight out of a fairy tale. Tia was elated to show her first-ever terracotta horse to her grandmother.

"Grandmaa!" she called out. "Come and look what I've made."

Gayatri Devi, who was making the bed, came out to see what Tia was talking about. When she saw the terracotta horse, she was unable to believe her eyes and thought there never was a terracotta sculpture so perfectly made. "My goodness!" gasped the old woman. "Child, how did you make such a wonderful horse? Even I couldn't have done it."

Tia was happy to be praised by her grandmother. "I'm glad you like it, Grandma," she said, smiling proudly.

"Now do come inside and get some sleep, you restless girl," said Gayatri Devi. "Children shouldn't stay up so late."

"Yes, Grandma," said Tia, yawning as she was very tired. "Good night." She put out the light and lay down beside her grandmother. A gentle breeze wafted the scent of freshly bloomed Rajnigandha flowers in through the open window, and the crickets chirped out in the dewy yard.

At midnight, Tia was awakened by a strange clip-clop sound. "What can it be?" she wondered, rubbing her eyes. As it was a windy night, she thought it was the wind beating against the door and went back to sleep. After a few minutes, she heard the clip-clop sound again, this time clearer than before. Tia realized that it was not the wind. Her grandmother was fast asleep, so she did not hear anything.

Tia got up from the bed and went out to see where the sound was coming from. She went to the krishnachura tree under which she had kept her terracotta horse, but the horse was no longer there. "Where could it have gone?" Tia wondered with her eyes wide open.

Celebrating Rakhi Festival with Tarak

The terracotta horse could not have moved anywhere by itself, and neither her parents nor her grandmother had moved it. "Oh no! It must have been stolen," Tia thought sadly. Just then, she heard the sound of the horse's hooves behind her. As she turned around, she saw the terracotta horse strolling along the grassy part of the yard! Tia rubbed her eyes and pinched herself to make sure that she was not dreaming.

The horse came walking toward her and greeted her with a friendly bow. "Thank you very much for giving me life," said the terracotta horse. "I'm so happy to be alive."

Tia was astonished to see the terracotta horse walking and speaking. "How can you move and talk?" she asked in surprise. "You can't possibly be the terracotta horse I made!"

"Your passion and dedication have given life to me," The horse replied, his eyes gleaming with life.

"That's so amazing!" Tia gasped, collecting her thoughts. She had always wished for a brother with whom she could play. "Your eyes are shining like the stars, so I shall call you Tarak."

The terracotta horse nodded his head in approval of the name, but he requested Tia not to tell anyone about his magical powers. It was hard for Tia to keep secrets, as she had a habit of sharing everything with her grandmother. "My grandma is very nice," she said. "I'm sure she would be happy to know you."

"I wish I could live in this house as a member of your family, but I will lose my life if you tell anyone about me," Tarak said with a sad look in his eyes.

Although Tia wanted to introduce her new friend to her grandmother, she could not put Tarak at risk of losing his life. Fighting against her habit, she promised to keep his secret. She further told Tarak about her family and apprised him of the neighborhood. Tarak already seemed to know everything about the neighborhood from a deeper perspective than other inhabitants. Tia was surprised at Tarak's perfect knowledge about the town.

"I know this place quite well since I was made from its soil," said Tarak.

Tia told him that the next day was Rakhi Purnima, the festival that celebrates the bond between brothers and sisters. The two of them kept talking to each other until the sky turned rosy. "I must go back now," said Tia, looking at the eastern sky. "Grandma wakes up very early, you see."

Tarak returned to his former place under the dawn-lit red tree, and Tia slipped into bed beside her grandmother. She was so tired that she could not get up before eight o'clock. Gayatri Devi thought it was because of the hard work she had done the previous day. The first thought that came to Tia's mind when she woke up was Tarak, her new friend and brother.

After freshening up, Tia sat down to make a rakhi out of colorful beads and silk threads. She wanted to give the most beautiful rakhi to her brother, so she made it with utmost care. When it was finished, she went to show it to her grandmother and sought her help to prepare a plate for the special occasion.

"Who are you doing all this for, dear?" her grandmother asked, putting down the vase she was painting. "You don't have a brother."

"Now I do have a brother, and it's none other than my dear Tarak," said Tia, pointing at the terracotta horse with a bright smile.

"Oh dear, it must be so lonely for you to be an only child," said Gayatri Devi.

"I wish I could introduce you to Tarak, but I must keep mum about him," Tia said in her mind.

Gayatri Devi felt sorry for her lonely granddaughter, so she agreed to her request. Together they prepared a beautiful plate with sandalwood paste, rice grains, scutch grass, paddy grains, an earthen lamp, and a peanut jaggery bar. Tia enthusiastically brought the arranged plate to

Tarak. She applied a mark on his forehead with the sandalwood paste and fed him a piece of peanut jaggery bar. At last, she tied the handmade rakhi on the forelimb of the terracotta horse. Gayatri Devi fondly watched her little granddaughter celebrate the festival of Rakhi with her imaginary brother.

Tia was eager to play with her terracotta horse, but she had to finish her daily tasks first. She had enough time to play with Tarak, since she did not have to attend school for two weeks due to renovation work. Being a diligent student, she had already finished most of her homework. She had only one assignment left to complete, a report on some of the most famous places in India. She wanted to visit the amazing places she was reading about, but she knew it was impossible. Her family could not afford to go on a tour of the country. As soon as she had finished her daily tasks, she took the terracotta horse to her playroom and shut the door. Then she asked Tarak how he felt about the rakhi she had tied on his forelimb.

"Oh I love it!" the horse replied happily. "It makes me feel special. Thank you so much for everything you've done for me today."

"It's my pleasure, Tarak," said Tia. "I used to feel so lonely on this occasion as I didn't have a brother, but now I have you."

Despite their cheerful interactions, Tarak noticed a worried look on Tia's face. "Dear Tia, if anything is bothering you, please feel free to share it with me."

After a moment's hesitation, Tia replied, "Well, you see, I have to prepare a project about some of the most famous places in India. I want to visit the places, but I don't have the means to do so."

"Leave it to me, Tia," said Tarak with a twinkle in his eyes. "I can take you on a tour of India. Will you give me the honor of being your tour guide?"

"Oh, really?" said Tia, her eyes lighting up for a moment. "It would be a dream come true, but I don't want to give you any trouble."

"You don't need to worry about me. I'm stronger than I look, you know. Besides, I owe you a gift for the rakhi," said Tarak.

Tia happily accepted Tarak's invitation and started making a list of the places she wanted to visit for her assignment. "I can pay the entry fees of the places with the money I've saved up in my piggy bank," said Tia, taking out an owl-shaped money bank made of terracotta.

"That's good," Tarak said with a nod. They planned to set out on their tour at 3 pm the next day when everyone would be taking their afternoon siesta. At dinner time, Tia brought some fresh green grass and peanut jaggery bars for Tarak, who relished the meal. She was so excited for the next day that she hardly slept a wink that night.

Exploring East India

The next morning, Tia woke up early to finish her daily tasks. She impatiently waited for the clock to strike three. When everyone had retired to their beds to take an afternoon nap, Tia ran to her playroom where Tarak stood waiting for her.

"So are you ready for the trip?" asked Tarak, shaking his mane to warm up.

"Yes! I've brought the list and my piggy bank," replied Tia, "but there's still a problem."

"Oh, what is it now?" Tarak asked.

"What if the others wake up before we return?"

"You don't have to worry about that. My neigh can lull everyone to deep sleep, so they will not wake up before our return." Saying this, the terracotta horse let out a long, spellbinding neigh. Tia had never heard such an amazing neigh before. "Where would you like to go first?" Tarak asked after the grown-ups had slipped into a deep slumber.

"Let's start with the Howrah Bridge," said Tia as she went through the list she had prepared. "I've seen a very beautiful picture of the bridge in my book. I would love to see it in person, but how will we reach there?"

"We will get there in no time. All you have to do is hop on my back," said Tarak, offering his back to the little girl.

"But can I go on a tour dressed like this?" asked Tia, looking at her usual calf-length cotton dress with grass and clay stains.

"No worries, we will be invisible to others," Tarak reassured her.

Little Tia was thrilled at the idea of being invisible. Without further ado, she climbed on Tarak's back. A cloud of golden dust rose around them as the terracotta horse neighed again and took a magical leap. Tia was a bit nervous, so she tightly held onto Tarak's back.

When the dust cleared, Tia found herself standing on the footpath of the Howrah Bridge with Tarak. "We have reached our destination!" Tarak declared. Tia's eyes widened at the marvelous sight resembling a scene from television. The bustling bridge with busy pedestrians, blue buses, yellow taxis, and numerous other vehicles presented a striking contrast to the calm waters of the Hooghly River flowing underneath. The steel beams overhead created intricate patterns of shadows on the bridge, and a cool breeze blew. "The Howrah Bridge is called the gateway to the city of joy, Kolkata," Tarak explained to Tia, who listened with interest. "You'd be surprised to know that this great bridge was made by steel riveting, without nuts and bolts. It was renamed Rabindra Setu, after the revered Bengali poet, Rabindranath Tagore."

On the banks, Tia could see people bathing and collecting the river's waters. The Dakshineshwar Kali temple, located on the eastern bank of the river, could be seen from the Howrah Bridge. The terracotta horse also showed her the second Hooghly bridge, Vidyasagar Setu, named after the great Indian polymath, Ishwar Chandra Vidyasagar. "There you can see the longest cable-stayed bridge in India," said Tarak, showing the mentioned bridge to the bright-eyed little tourist.

Tia spotted several ferry boats, loaded with passengers, floating dreamily on the Hooghly River. In her heart, she wished to take a ferry ride. "Let's take a flight over the river!" suggested her terracotta companion. Tia happily agreed to this enticing suggestion. "Hold on tight," said Tarak as they took flight and flew over the sunlit river.

"It's even more fun than a ferry ride," said Tia, taking in the wonderful view of the Howrah Bridge and the Hooghly River with her sparkling eyes.

When it was time for them to go back home, Tarak neighed, taking a magical leap again. They were surrounded by sparkling dust, and in a moment they were back home. As Tarak's magic wore off, Tia's parents and grandmother awoke from their siesta. Before going to sleep, Tia wrote down everything she had learned from Tarak during their trip in a notebook. She intended to record the memories of their magic trips. She expressed her gratitude to Tarak by feeding him his favorite foods, peanut jaggery bars and fresh grass.

On the next day, Tia and Tarak planned to visit the Sundarbans mangrove forest. "I've heard many interesting stories about the Sundarbans," Tia said in the afternoon when her family had gone to lie down.

"Well, then, what are we waiting for?" Tarak asked with a gleam in his eyes. "Hop on my back, and I'll take you where you want to go."

Tia cheerfully followed the instructions of her guide. The terracotta horse let out a neigh that sent everyone to deep sleep, and then he took an extraordinary leap. They were once more surrounded by a cloud of magic dust.

Soon, they alighted in one of the watchtowers in the Sundarbans mangrove. "Here we are in the highest watchtower of the Sundarbans, from where you can see the famous royal Bengal tigers and other wild animals," said Tarak. Little Tia found herself completely captured by the view of the mangrove forest intersected by waterways reflecting the greenery. There was a sweet water pond nearby, where spotted deer, Indian grey mongooses, and hairy wild boars were drinking water. Tia also spotted some birds she had never seen in her hometown. She could not stop herself from mimicking some of their calls. Tarak told Tia about the various species of birds including small minivet, mangrove whistler, cinnamon bittern, brown fish owl, purple sunbird, and waterfowls found in the Sundarban National Park. "The Sundarban is the world's largest delta, formed by the joining of the rivers, Ganga, Brahmaputra, and Meghna in the Bay of Bengal. Do you know why the Sundarban is so named?"

"Yes, because it's a beautiful forest, right?" said Tia, referring to the Bengali meaning of the phrase.

"You're right, but there's another reason," said Tarak. "It was named after the large mangrove trees called Sundari that grow here."

"Oh, I see!" Tia said with a curious look in her sparkling, dark eyes. Suddenly, the birds started chirping louder, and the animals that were drinking water in the pond moved away quickly. Tia was surprised to see the strange behavior of the birds and animals. "What's wrong?"

she asked curiously. Then a majestic royal Bengal tiger with flame-colored fur and coal-black stripes came into sight. The tiger opened his large mouth and let out a thunderous roar that made Tia's heart pound.

"There's the national animal of India," Tarak said to an excited Tia. "You must be aware that the tiger is the symbol of power, valor, and grace." Tia gazed at the magnificent tiger with her eyes wide open.

Then Tarak took her to the bank of an estuary, where they caught sight of a pod of elusive dolphins jumping out of the waters. What a lovely sight it was! "They are so adorable," gasped Tia.

"They are the Gangetic river dolphins," said Tarak. "Do you know that the river dolphin is the national aquatic animal of India?"

"No, I didn't know that dolphins could live in rivers," said Tia.

"Because of the sound of their breathing, they are also called Susu or Shushuk in Bengali. This rare species can only survive in freshwater. Unfortunately, they are threatened by water pollution and decreased flow of freshwater," said Tarak. Saddened to hear this, Tia resolved to do everything in her power to prevent water pollution and the extinction of these wonderful creatures.

"Now, let's go and see the saltwater crocodiles," said Tarak. He took her to the banks of a creek, where nine crocodiles lay basking in the afternoon sun. The largest of them seemed to be grinning at them because of its protruding teeth. "The saltwater crocodile is known as the dragon of the Sundarbans since it's the largest reptile on earth," explained Tarak. The immensity of the crocodiles astonished little Tia.

She wanted to see the Sundarbans' dragons up close. As she was watching the crocodiles, her silver anklet got loosened and fell down. It got stuck in a bush near the mouth of a crocodile. "Oh no, my anklet!" cried Tia. Her high-pitched voice alerted the crocodiles. She took a broken branch floating nearby and reached into the bush cautiously. The crocodile was surprised to see the branch hovering in the air since Tia was invisible. He grabbed the branch in his large mouth, making Tia lose her balance. The terracotta horse swiftly lifted Tia onto his back. Fortunately, Tia managed to get hold of her anklet before the crocodile could reach them, and the two friends flew away.

The next moment, Tia found herself in the yard of her house. "That was close," sighed Tia. Oblivious of Tia's adventures, her family woke up from their afternoon slumber and went through their evening routines. At night, Tia dreamed of all the amazing things Tarak had shown her that day.

The following afternoon, they went to visit Darjeeling according to Tia's list. As they arrived at their destination, Tia found herself in a most beautiful place surrounded by hills wrapped in snow-white clouds. She could hear the soothing sound of falling water. "We are now inside the Rock Garden at Chunnu Summer Falls," Tarak explained.

"Oh, I feel like I'm in a fairy tale!" said Tia, looking around with fascination.

"This place is known as Rock Garden because of the special seating arrangements made of rocks," said Tarak. Tia was spellbound by the beauty of the refreshing greenery, hilly streams, and fascinating flowers of different species.

"Now let me take you to another interesting place," suggested the terracotta horse, offering his back to the eager little girl. As they arrived at the place, Tarak told Tia, "We are now in the Padmaja Naidu Zoological Park. It's considered to be one of the best zoos in the world as it gives shelter to exotic Himalayan wildlife species like red pandas, Tibetan wolves, Indian tigers, black bears, and snow leopards."

Tia was eager to see the animals mentioned by Tarak. They were fortunate to be able to see all the attractions of the zoo within the available time. Tia enjoyed watching all the animals, and she quickly developed a soft spot for the adorable, fluffy red pandas.

Then the terracotta horse took her to the Nightingale Park from where the snow-covered mountains could be seen. Tia sat on one of the park benches with colorful shades to enjoy the scenic beauty of the Nightingale Park. In the middle of the park, she saw a circular stage. Tarak told her that the stage was used by the locals for performing cultural programmes. He showed her the beautiful waterfalls coming from the top of the Shiva Temple and a wonderful musical fountain adorning the landscape. The park looked like a silvery-green wonderland in Tia's eyes. When the mist cleared, They saw the majestic peak of Kanchenjunga. Tia was mesmerized by the view of the heavenly mountain, but Tarak's explanation aroused her from her reverie. "That's the third highest mountain in the world, lying in the eastern Himalayas," said the terracotta horse.

"Oh I see," muttered Tia, "but what does the name Kanchenjunga mean?"

"It can be translated as the 'Five Treasures of the Snow' with reference to its five peaks," replied Tarak.

"It sounds so interesting!" Tia said dreamily.

"Would you like to see the mountains from up close?" Tarak asked, although he already knew what Tia's answer would be.

"Yes, I'd love to!" said the little girl, her eyes glowing with excitement.

They flew amid the clouds over misty mountains and lush green tea gardens where workers were collecting tender tea leaves in their baskets. They flew over the colorful houses, winding roads, and the clock tower which played a lovely tune as the clock struck four. The sky was suddenly overcast, and it started raining. Thanks to the protective layer of warmth Tarak had created around them, they did not get wet. Tia tightened her grip around Tarak as a bolt of lightning flashed across the sky.

"Did you know that the word Darjeeling means 'Land of Thunderbolt' in the Tibetan language?"

The little girl shook her head in surprise. As she absorbed Tarak's words, another bolt of lightning struck, forcing them to return home.

Exploring North India

The subsequent afternoon, they went on a trip to the Taj Mahal in the city of Agra. The pearly white marble mausoleum on the banks of the Yamuna River seemed like a mirage. The four minarets, the neat rows of cypress trees, and the lush green gardens created a picture-perfect scene. Tarak showed Tia the dreamy reflection of the monument in the lotus pond, which looked like an identical monument in an alternate dimension.

"The Taj Mahal is one of the seven wonders of the world, you know," said Tarak. "It was built by the Mughal emperor, Shah Jahan in memory of his beloved wife, Mumtaz Mahal."

Tia felt like she was standing in front of a fairy palace. She bumped into some tourists as they made their way into the monument. Thanks to their invisibility and the crowd, no one noticed them.

Fascinated, Tia gazed at the gorgeous interiors embellished with floral paintings. She was able to identify the various kinds of flowers preserved inside the marble walls, never to wilt. Being a simple town girl, the luxurious lifestyle of the Mughals seemed like a fairy tale to her.

The main dome with its unique mechanism of echoes doubled Tia's excitement. The words that came out of her lips lingered in the mystical air for quite a long time. "It feels like we are talking to the monument," said Tia, feeling special as the chamber echoed their names multiple times.

Tarak was amused at Tia's dreamy notion. "So now you know why Taj Mahal is considered to be the most beautiful building in the world," said the terracotta horse when they had completed their tour of the famous historical monument.

On the next day, they went to see the Golden Temple in Amritsar, a city in the state of Punjab. Following the custom of the temple, Tia covered her head with an orange scarf that she had brought from home. She was immediately fascinated by the magnificence of the golden structure, which glittered in the afternoon sun. The large pool surrounding the temple created a spellbinding effect, making Tia think that the temple was floating in the water. "The pool you see around the temple is known as the Amrit Sarovar, which means the pool of nectar," explained Tarak.

"I see!" Tia said in amazement. She washed her hands and bare feet in the lake before they entered the temple.

"The Golden Temple is the most famous shrine in Sikhism. It was built by Guru Arjan. You'd be amazed to know that this temple has the world's largest free kitchen or Langar!" Tarak said. As they walked into the aromatic langar hall, Tia saw people from various backgrounds sitting in long rows and enjoying a delicious vegetarian meal. "Although we couldn't eat at the langar, I've had a great time at the Golden Temple!" a pleased Tia told Tarak when they were back home.

The next destination on Tia's list was Shimla, the capital of Himachal Pradesh, so they went there the next day. Tia could not have imagined a more beautiful place. She felt fortunate to be able to experience the magical beauty of Shimla in person. "We have now arrived at The Ridge road, which attracts countless numbers of tourists as you can see," Tarak told an amazed Tia, who looked around at all the sparkling cafés, restaurants, showrooms, and shops with her wide eyes. She could also see the snow-capped mountain peaks. "Shimla is known as the queen of the hills for its scenic beauty. This hill station is one of the most popular holiday destinations in the world," Tarak explained.

The terracotta horse showed her the celebrated Gaiety Theater, which is the center of all cultural activities in Shimla. Tia was amazed by the architectural style of the Gaiety Theater as she had never seen a building like it before. Tarak informed her that it was designed by the renowned English architect, Henry Irwin in gothic architectural style.

"Tarak, what are the famous hills of Shimla?" Tia asked as the question suddenly popped into her curious head.

"That's what I was about to tell you," said Tarak. "Shimla is situated on seven hills, namely Jakhoo Hill, Elysium Hill, Inveram Hill, Prospect Hill, Observatory Hill, Summer Hill, and Bantony Hill."

"Which of them is the highest?" asked Tia, her interest piqued by the seven hills.

"Jakhoo Hill is the highest peak in Shimla," Tarak replied. "Let's go there!"

Tia learned that the Jakhoo Hill is famous for an ancient temple dedicated to Lord Hanuman. Although Tarak could easily fly up to the hilltop, Tia wanted to enjoy the short trek, climbing through the ancient deodar trees. Near the temple, Tia saw a troop of monkeys getting fed by the people. As some monkeys were fighting over food, a little monkey fell from a tree branch. Fortunately, Tia caught him before he hit the ground. Astonished to see this marvel, the monkeys stopped fighting. "There you go!" Tia whispered as the little monkey went away to his mother, who was nearby. Tia was glad to have been able to save the monkey from getting hurt. None of the tourists noticed what happened.

Beholding the colossal orange-colored statue of Lord Hanuman made Tia feel so tiny. The hilltop provided them with a breathtaking view of the Himalayas. They concluded their trip with a magical flight over the snow-covered Himalayas.

Exploring West India

The next day, they were going to start exploring the western part of India. The fourth place on Tia's list was Jaisalmer, so the terracotta horse took her there.

"We have arrived at the famed golden city, in the heart of the Thar desert," said Tarak. "As you already know, Jaisalmer is one of the most remarkable tourist attractions of Rajasthan. It's known as the golden city because of its golden sandstone architecture." Tia gazed at all the golden-hued houses in wonder.

They went to the sprawling Jaisalmer Fort, situated on the top of the Trikuta hill, surrounded by the Thar Desert. "This fort was built by the Rajput ruler, Rawal Jaisal from whom the monument gets its name," Tarak explained. "Once the scene of many battles, it is now the residence of a quarter of the city's population. The fort is popularly known as Sonar Kila or the golden fort."

Tia was entranced by the grandeur of this ancient monument, which stood against the ravages of time. "It must be so wonderful to live here," said Tia. Then a question came to her mind. "Is this fort made of sand?" she asked her terracotta guide.

"Not really," Tarak corrected her. "It's made of yellow sandstone."

The four splendid entrance gates, dreamy alleyways, and royal palaces transported Tia to the bygone era. Tarak apprised her of the magnificent Jain temples and the Lakshminath Temple that added to the glory of the fort.

Then the terracotta horse took Tia on a magical ride through the sand dunes. She spotted a string of traditionally decorated camels carrying tourists on their backs. Tia felt like she was in the world of the Arabian Nights. The beauty of the sand dunes was enhanced by the light of the evening sun. When they came near a natural well, Tia decided to write their names in the sand. As she was doing so, her delicate feet sunk into the sand, and she lost her balance. "Tia, don't move!" Tarak warned her. "It's quicksand."

"Help!" cried Tia, who had already sunk to her waist. "How can I get out of here?" Tarak quickly dove into the sand. "Tarak, where are you?" Tia asked, getting more nervous. Soon she felt Tarak's back lifting her out of the quicksand. Catching her breath, Tia hugged her companion. She did manage to write "Tia and Tarak" on the sand before returning home. Back in the yard of her home, Tia could still feel the ambience of the golden city. "I'll never forget this day," she thought with a pounding heart.

The next afternoon, the two friends went to visit the Gir National Park in the state of Gujarat. Tia observed the large and dry deciduous forest with curiosity as Tarak told her about the Asiatic lions that live there. It had always been Tia's dream to see a real lion. "Did you know that it's the only home to the endangered Asiatic lion?" Tarak asked.

"Yes, I've heard it from my teacher," replied Tia.

"It's also known as Sasan Gir. There are seven major perennial rivers in Gir. Wouldn't you like to know their names?" Tarak asked an inattentive Tia. She looked for the lions among the blackbucks, Chinkara, four-horned antelope, nilgai, and the Indian leopard.

"Tarak, where are the lions?" Tia asked impatiently. "I don't want to go back home before seeing a lion." After wandering for a while, they spotted a majestic golden lioness playing with her three cubs under a large banyan tree. The lioness looked so calm and affectionate that for a moment, Tia forgot she was looking at the most formidable predator on Earth. The cubs were playing with a small twig that broke, interrupting their game. Tia saw another twig lying at a distance and went to pick it up. As she approached the lion cubs, their mother let out a loud yawn, which exposed her large canines. Tia's heart throbbed, and shivers ran down her spine. The cubs accepted the offered twig and started playing with it. Watching them play with the twig, Tia regained her composure.

"Are you happy now that you've seen the lions up close?" asked Tarak.

"Yes, I am," beamed Tia as they concluded their exciting trip.

The following afternoon, the duo decided to visit Goa, a state on the west coast of India. Tia found herself on a scenic beach lined with towering palm trees and large, muticolored umbrellas under which the bathers chatted. The little girl could not take her eyes off the enchanting view of the Arabian Sea. "We're in Calangute Beach, the queen of beaches in Goa," said Tarak.

Tia rapturously watched the colorful parachutes soaring in the azure sky and the tourists engaging in various watersports. She dipped her toes in the pristine waters of the Arabian Sea and made sand castles as the cool sea breeze brushed her face and ruffled her wavy hair. Walking along the glistening beach with Tarak, she spotted two pretty shells lying on the golden sand. She managed to pick them up before the waves crashed against the shore. "Let's keep them as souvenirs!" said Tia.

Tarak showed her the centuries-old Aguada Fort and the lighthouse overlooking the sea. Next, the terracotta horse took her to the oldest church of Goa, the Basilica of Bom Jesus. Inside the church, Tia was awed by the glimmering gemstones and gilded alter. "This church contains the mortal remains of Goa's patron saint, St. Francis Xavier," Tarak said, showing her the sacred mummy lying inside a silver casket from a distance.

They went to see the Dudhsagar Waterfalls located on the Mandovi River. True to its name which means "Sea of Milk", the waterfall looked like milk falling from the hills. Playful monkeys gamboled in the surrounding trees, and bright-colored birds chirped in the branches as if singing the glories of the place. Fascinated by the beauty of the waterfall, Tia felt like joining the birds in singing its praise.

"Here we are at the fifth-highest waterfall in India!" Tarak said to an amazed Tia, who could not wait to touch the sparkling waters. The big carps frolicking below the waterfall tickled her bare little feet, making her laugh out loud.

On their trip, they saw two elephants taking a bath in the river with some people. Tia wished she could play with the elephants. "But they can't see us of course," she thought wistfully. As they were about to leave, one of the elephants turned in their direction and playfully splashed water at them. "How can he see us?" asked Tia, laughing.

"I think he can smell us," said Tarak as they leaped toward home.

Exploring South India

On the next day, the two friends began their tour of southern India with the Swiflet Cave of Munnar in Kerala. "Wow!" gasped Tia, her breath held by the enormous cave dotted with thousands of birds and their unique, well-built nests containing eggs and nestlings. "I have never seen such a large number of birds before!"

"These birds are called swiflets," said Tarak as Tia looked around excitedly. "They are the main attraction of this famous cave."

Knowing how much Tia loves birds, Tarak let her watch the swiflets and enjoy the natural beauty of the place in her own way. While exploring the large cave, Tia's eyes fell on a quivering egg. "Tarak, look! The egg is about to hatch," said Tia as she watched tiny cracks appear in the eggshell. The cracks widened, and a cute baby swiflet popped out of the cracked egg.

"Welcome to the world!" Tia and Tarak chimed in unison, even though the bird could not see them. For a moment, Tia wished to adopt the baby swiflet and take it home with her. But then she realized that it would not be the right thing to do.

"You'd be happier here with your family and friends," thought Tia as she waved goodbye to the hatchling.

The next day late in the afternoon, the duo went to visit Madurai, a famous city situated on the banks of the Vaigai River in Tamil Nadu. Tia had her breath taken away by the colorful, majestic gateway towers dominating the skyline of this ancient city. "There are fourteen of them!" gasped Tia.

"They are the gopurams or gateway towers of the famous Meenakshi Amman Temple," said Tarak. Tia saw various intricate carvings that depicted mythological stories from ancient Indian texts. She remembered hearing some of them from her grandmother. They went to the southern bank of the river where the temple stood. Tia was so engrossed that she almost bumped into a pillar. At the centre of the temple, a beautiful pond with a golden lotus caught Tia's eyes. "It is the golden lily pond where there are no fish," Tarak explained to a curious Tia. While beholding the presiding deities of the temple, Tia was happy to see the beautiful idol of Goddess Meenakshi holding a parrot in one hand.

Before returning home, Tia found herself spellbound by the grandeur of the temple halls, especially the dazzling Hall of Thousand Pillars built out of one rock. "I can never forget our trip to Madurai!" said Tia as she and Tarak returned home. That night, she listened to myths and legends about parrots from her grandmother.

The following afternoon, Tarak took Tia on a trip to Mysore, a historical city in the state of Karnataka. "Do you know that Mysore is known as the city of palaces?" Tarak asked. "The city is home to seven palaces, including the Mysore Palace."

"Wow! Mysore seems to be a wonderful city," Tia said with anticipation.

They flew to the magnificent Mysore Palace, situated in the heart of the city, facing the Chamundi Hills in the east. The majestic palace with pink marble domes and beautiful arches stood like a dreamy gateway to the glorious past. "It's the residence of Mysore's royal family, the Wadiyar dynasty," Tarak informed Tia.

Much to Tia's delight, they entered the palace through the Dolls' Pavilion which displayed a beautiful collection of traditional dolls and sculptures including a wooden elephant decorated with gold. "What a lovely collection!" she whispered. Inside the palace, the large chandeliers, beautiful carvings, antique furniture, ancient portraits, and stunning works of art put Tia under a spell. She came out of the spell as a tourist accidentally stepped on her toe. But soon she found herself captivated by the grand halls including the gold and blue Durbar Hall and the Kalyan Mandap or wedding hall with peacock motifs. The two friends concluded their southern trip with a tour of the exquisite garden surrounding the palace.

Tia still could not believe that she had been to so many beautiful places with Tarak. Watching the western sky, she realized that it was time to go back home. "Thanks for making my dreams come true, Tarak," said Tia as she climbed on Tarak's back with a satisfied heart. But the cloud of magic dust that rose with the terracotta horse's neigh looked thinner than usual. And for the first time, Tarak failed to take the perfect leap. "Are you alright, Tarak?" Tia asked, worried.

"Ah, yes, I'm all right," The terracotta horse replied. "I was just distracted." Tarak tried to leap again, but he failed, making Tia concerned.

"What if we can't go back home?" Tia thought anxiously. After several failed attempts, the terracotta horse finally succeeded in taking the magic leap that transported them home. On reaching home, Tarak fell to the ground, exhausted. "Tarak, are you hurt?" Tia cried, helping him get up.

Fortunately, the terracotta horse was not broken. "I'm fine, Tia," Tarak replied, breathing heavily. "Don't worry about me."

Tia knew that something was wrong with her best friend. "If you think of me as your sister and best friend, then please tell me the truth," Tia insisted.

After a moment's hesitation, Tarak replied, "I think I've used up my magical powers to travel, so I may not be able to take you anywhere again."

Tia was sad to hear this, but she tried to remain cheerful in front of Tarak. "Don't worry, Tarak," said Tia. "I'm sure you will feel better after a good night's rest." After feeding Tarak with a banana and some fresh grass, she let him rest.

The next day, a tourist came to buy terracotta souvenirs from them. Tarak stood watching Tia and her father as they attended to the customer. Soon, the man's eyes fell on the unique terracotta horse. "What a wonderful work of art!" he said, looking at Tarak with admiration. "I'm sure my son would love it." He offered to pay a large amount of money for the remarkable terracotta sculpture. Tarak did not want to be sold off, but he knew it was his fate. Moreover, he realized that he was no longer useful to Tia.

But the little girl did not want to be separated from her best friend. She earnestly requested her father not to sell Tarak. Gangaram did not want to hurt his daughter's feelings. Watching Tia's love for the terracotta horse, her family had started considering Tarak as a family member too, despite being unaware of his magical powers.

"Sorry to disappoint you, Sir," Gangaram said to the customer politely. "But this terracotta horse is not for sale. Please feel free to choose another one."

"That's such a pity," the man said, looking a bit upset. Since there were many terracotta sculptures to choose from, he soon gave up on Tarak and picked another horse. Gangaram offered it at a discount to the customer, who received it happily. When the tourist went away, Tia thanked her father for not selling her beloved terracotta horse. Tarak was touched by Tia's unconditional love for him.

"Thank you so much for not giving me up," Tarak told Tia when she brought him dinner.

"How can I give you up, Tarak?" Tia said. "Look what you have for dinner today!"

"My favorite peanut jaggery bars!" Tarak said cheerfully as he dug in.

After having a few bites, the terracotta horse started emanating a warm golden light, but he was unaware of this. "Wow! You're glowing, Tarak!" gasped Tia.

"Huh? What's happening to me?" Tarak wondered. "I feel as light and energetic as I did when I came into existence."

"It's the peanut jaggery bar!" exclaimed Tia as she finally realized why Tarak had lost his powers. "You haven't had it for two days."

"Ah! Why didn't I think of it? The peanut jaggery bar is the source of my powers!" said Tarak. Tia happily hugged Tarak who lifted him on his back.

"I'll make sure we never run out of your peanut jaggery bars again," said Tia. The two best friends laughed happily, looking forward to many more adventures to share.

Not only did Tia make a lot of wonderful memories with Tarak, but also the best project in her class. For her great work, Tia received a certificate to which she added Tarak's name.

About the Author

Adrita Goswami

Adrita Goswami is a published author of children's books and co-author of several anthologies. She began spinning tales of fantasy and adventure when she was six and wrote her first book, A World Beyond The Rainbow at the age of thirteen. Apart from writing, Adrita enjoys reading, painting, listening to music, and spending time in nature. She is presently working on her upcoming books.

www.ingramcontent.com/pod-product-compliance
Lightning Source LLC
La Vergne TN
LVHW041602070526
838199LV00046B/2098